Echo and the Bat Pack

KING TUT'S GRANDMOTHER

text by Roberto Pavanello

translated by Marco Zeni

STONE ARCH BOOKS

a capstone imprint

First published in the United States in 2012
by Stone Arch Books
A Capstone Imprint
1710 Roe Crest Drive
North Mankato, Minnesota 56003
www.capstonepub.com

Text by Roberto Pavanello
Original cover and illustrations by Blasco Pisapiam, Pamela Brughera, and Alessandro Muscillo
Graphic Project by Laura Zuccotti and Gioia Giunchi

© 2007 Edizioni Piemme S.p.A., via Tiziano 32 - 20145 Milano- Italy
International Rights © Atlantyca S.p.A., via Leopardi, 8 — 20123 Milano, Italy — foreignrights@atlantyca.it

Original Title: LA NONNA DI TUTANKHAMON

Translation by: Marco Zeni

www.batpat.it

LIbrary of Congress Cataloging-in-Publication Data is available on the Library of Congress website.

ISBN: 978-1-4342-4245-7 (hardcover)
ISBN: 978-1-4342-3823-8 (library binding)

Summary: The Bat Pack discovers that the mummy in Fogville's museum isn't quite as dead as they expected...

Designer: Emily Harris

Printed in China
0412/CA21200581
042012   006679

TABLE OF CONTENTS

HELLO THERE!

I'm your friend Echo, here to tell you about one of the Bat Pack's adventures!

Do you know what I do for a living? I'm a writer, and scary stories are my specialty. Creepy stories about witches, ghosts, and graveyards. But I'll tell you a secret — I am a real scaredy-bat!

First of all, let me introduce you to the Bat Pack. These are my friends. . . .

Becca

Age: 10

Loves all animals (especially bats!)

Excellent at bandaging broken wings

Michael

Age: 12

Smart, thoughtful, and good at solving problems

Doesn't take no for an answer

Tyler

Age: 11

Computer genius

Funny and adventurous, but scared of his own shadow

Dear fans of scary stories,

Do you like stories about ancient Egypt? I love them! As a matter of fact, I am a real Egypt buff. My cousin Alec, who lives in Egypt, is the one who first got me interested in ancient Egypt. You see, he's an Egyptian fruit bat, so he knows *all* about Egypt. What is an Egyptian fruit bat, you ask? It is a large bat that feeds entirely on fruits and vegetables. My cousin even eats spinach and Brussels sprouts! What's with that face? Don't you like them? Cousin Alec always says, "Vegetables and fruit will make you grow by a foot!"

Anyway, it was my cousin who first told me all about Egypt, and since then I have read a lot of books about Egyptian history, especially about mummies.

Ah, mummies. Fascinating topic, isn't it? I used to think so too. At least until I lived through the story I'm about to tell you. . . .

Chapter 1

Sunstroke?

The Silver family is always taking me on new adventures and introducing me to new things. And why not? I'm practically part of the family! One afternoon, Mr. and Mrs. Silver decided that the family should spend a nice day at Placid Lake. I was so excited!

Unfortunately, that day I discovered that I get seasick — or rather, *lakesick*. The endless rocking of the boat made me so queasy! And don't even get me started on the sun. When will humans finally understand that bats don't like sunlight? Even wearing my sunglasses, hat, and sunscreen didn't help. And then Tyler decided to teach me how to fish.

"Look, Echo, it's easy," Tyler explained. "All you have to do is hold the fishing rod like this, release the reel, bend your arm backward, and throw!"

He handed me the rod. I carefully followed his instructions one by one. I even managed to do a nice throw. But I hadn't realized that I'd actually catch something!

"Hey! I have a bite!" I hollered, watching the bobber sink into the water. "Hurry up!"

"Pull! Pull!" Tyler yelled. "Reel it in!"

"I can't!" I protested. "It's too heavy!"

Tyler was about to help me when a powerful jerk pulled me right off the boat. I hit the water with a loud *splash*!

Michael, Becca, and Tyler immediately dove in to save me (by the way, I can't swim). Becca and Michael rescued me, while Tyler pulled his fishing rod out of the water. At the other end of the line was the catch of the day — an old tire.

After that, my fishing adventure was over. I spent the rest of the day on the shore, wrapped up in a towel.

On the car ride home, I lay sprawled out in the back, watching the boat trailer bounce up and down on the road behind us. Michael, Tyler, and Becca were all asleep in the back seat.

As a general rule, I don't like riding in the car. The first time the Silvers took me for a car ride, I discovered that I get carsick. Very carsick. I tried to stay in Becca's arms, but even that didn't help. Eventually I found out that I could lie in front of the rear window and lean back against the headrest. At least then I could look out of the window. Then Mr. Silver came

up with a brilliant idea. He had a tiny revolving seat installed in front of the rear window. It was the perfect place for me to sit.

Even though it was dark and I should have been full of energy, I was falling asleep. After all, Michael, Tyler, and Becca had been dozing for a while. Suddenly, something caught my attention. A white blur had crossed the road and disappeared into the woods.

I rubbed my eyes. *What was that?* I wondered.

A second later the white object reappeared and started chasing after us! I couldn't believe what I was seeing. It was a MUMMY!

The mummy's head was covered with long red hair, and its body was wrapped in white bandages that hung loosely from its arms and legs.

Scaredy-bat! I was petrified!

The mummy was holding its arms out
toward me and getting closer and closer to
the boat. I could see its ice-blue eyes
staring at me, full of anger.

I frantically
tried to wake up
Michael, Tyler,
and Becca,
but I was too
terrified
to speak.

All of a
sudden, the
mummy jumped
forward and tried to
get into the boat. Luckily, it
only managed to grab onto the back
of the boat. The trailer skidded across the road
crazily.

"HELP!!!" I finally managed to scream.

"What's the matter?" Becca asked, sleepily.

"Oh, nothing, kids," Mr. Silver reassured them. "I must have hit a pothole! Take a look back there, Echo. Is everything okay?"

"NO, IT'S NOT OKAY!" I yelled. "THERE'S A MUMMY HANGING ON TO OUR BOAT!"

A minute of silence followed. Then everybody burst into laughter.

"I think you might have gotten too much sun today, Echo!" Tyler said.

"I'm serious!" I insisted. "Look!"

The three kids turned around and looked at the boat.

"See?" I said.

"See what?" Michael asked.

I couldn't believe they couldn't see the mummy. Were they crazy? But when I turned around to look at the road, the mummy had vanished.

"B-but . . ." I stuttered. "I swear I saw it!"

"You'd better go to bed early tonight, Echo," Michael said. "And no night flights!"

Chapter 2

It's Just
Toilet Paper

I didn't sleep well that night. I dreamed that the mummy was following me around Fogville, while I couldn't even fly. Then someone grabbed my wing. The mummy had caught me!

I opened my eyes, and there it was. But it looked like . . . Becca? What was Becca doing in my attic?

"Relax, Echo, it was just a bad dream!" she whispered. "It's all over now."

But it wasn't. Just then, a real mummy — covered in bandages from head to toe — staggered into the room! It lurched toward us, growling.

I immediately jumped into Becca's arms, trying to hide. The mummy was getting closer and closer. Beneath its bandages I could clearly see its ... blond hair? Since when did mummies wear sweatshirts?

"Cut it out, Tyler!" Becca snapped. "Can't you see how much you're scaring him?"

"Tyler?" I asked, scared wingless. "Is that you?"

Laughing, Tyler started unraveling the toilet paper he'd wrapped himself up with. "Sorry, Echo," he said, still cracking up. "I just couldn't help myself."

"Don't let him bug you, Echo," Becca comforted me. "He's our brother, after all, not yours."

"Echo was right about the mummy, though," Michael said as he walked into the attic.

"Come on, Michael. Give it a break!" Becca told him.

"I'm serious," Michael said. "Dad just read an article in the *Fogville Echo* about a special exhibit at the city museum. The Ancient Egypt section is going to display the mummy of some important Egyptian queen."

"Are you serious?" I asked.

"Of course he is," Tyler said. "Maybe Her Majesty went for a walk last night and got lost! If we'd known, we could have given her a ride. It would have been so exciting!"

"There he goes again," Becca said with a sigh.

I hurried downstairs to ask Mr. Silver about the article. Michael, Tyler, and Becca all followed close behind. To everyone's surprise, Mr. Silver confirmed that both the news about the exhibit and the mummy were true.

"The mummy arrived on a special flight from Egypt the other day with some statues and ancient sarcophagi," Mr. Silver told us.

"Is she really a queen?" I asked.

"That's what the article says," Mr. Silver said. "Queen Tiye, wife of Amenhotep III."

"She can't be that famous," Tyler said. "I've never heard of her."

"If you want to know more about her, the exhibit is opening tomorrow afternoon," Mr. Silver told us. "Dr. Robert Templeton, the American Egyptologist who discovered Tiye's tomb, is giving a tour."

"I want to go!" I exclaimed. "I LOVE ancient Egypt!"

"Sorry, Echo," Mr. Silver said. "I'm afraid bats aren't allowed in the museum."

I was very disappointed to hear that. At least until Becca leaned over and whispered, "Don't worry, Echo. They can't keep you out if they can't see you. . . ."

Chapter 3

A Thousand-Year-Old Granny

The next day, Michael, Tyler, Becca, and I went to check out the new exhibit. Fogville's museum was enormous! Hidden in Becca's backpack, I could peek around without being seen. We followed the signs to an area labeled "Ancient Egypt."

When we turned the corner, we found ourselves in a hallway already crowded with people. Apparently we weren't the only ones interested in seeing the mummy! A dark-haired

man wearing a pair of round, metal-rimmed glasses stepped to the front of the room.

"Ladies and gentlemen," the professor began, smiling at his audience, "welcome to ancient Egypt! I am here with you today to tell you about an extraordinary person. A woman who lived almost 3,500 years ago, whose tomb I was lucky enough to discover: Queen Tiye. She was a great queen and, let me add, a great woman! The ladies who are here today can be proud of such an ancestor!"

"He's so charming!" Becca said.

"He looks like an older version of Michael," Tyler said, giggling to himself.

"Cut it out, Tyler," Michael said. "Can you at least try to behave like a normal person for a change?"

"Are you proud, Becca?" Tyler asked Becca.

He grinned at his sister. "Maybe one day you'll be a mummy too."

"And maybe one day you'll grow a brain!" she responded.

Cuddled up in Becca's bag, I giggled.

"Queen Tiye," the professor continued, "was the wife of Pharaoh Amenhotep III. Amenhotep was known as Egypt's 'Sun King' because of the

magnificent monuments he had built in Thebes, which was the capital of Egypt at that time. He became king when he was just eight years old and married Tiye when he was only 11!"

"Maybe I could be a pharaoh too!" I whispered to Becca.

"Maybe," Becca whispered back, "but no one would want to marry you!"

"While Amenhotep was still a child, his mother ruled the kingdom," Templeton continued. "However, when he finally ascended the throne, he wanted his beautiful, beloved wife by his side. Amenhotep loved Tiye so much that he even had an artificial lake and a garden built for her so that they could take walks together."

"That is so romantic!" Becca said with a sigh.

"Tiye was always there for her husband when he had to make important decisions," the

professor said. "When Amenhotep III died, she ruled Egypt, even after her son Amenhotep IV had ascended the throne."

"What a character!" I said from within the backpack.

"Amenhotep IV went on to marry the famous Queen Nefertiti, who gave him six children," Professor Templeton finished. "Unfortunately they were all girls."

"What do you mean, 'unfortunately'?" Becca burst out.

"I didn't mean to offend you, young lady," the professor said. He smiled gently. "You must understand that having a male child was very important for a king, so that he would have someone to succeed him on the throne."

"Well, that's silly," Becca said. I could tell she was still upset. "A girl could rule just as well as a boy."

"So what did he do?" Michael asked.

"One of Amenhotep's many other wives gave birth to a son," the professor explained. "That son would become the most famous pharaoh of all — Tutankhamen! You probably know him as King Tut."

"So Queen Tiye was Tutankhamen's grandmother," Michael said.

"That's correct!" the professor replied. "And as far as we know, she was the one responsible for his education and training as a future pharaoh."

"Jeez," Tyler muttered. "I'll have to ask my grandma to teach me a couple of her tricks."

"If you'll all follow me, we'll start our tour now," the professor instructed.

The other halls in the museum were a bit darker, so I snuck out of the backpack and hid underneath Becca's jacket. I could see much better from there.

The group stopped in front of a small painted plaster bust. "This is the only portrait we have of the Queen," the professor told us. "Notice the large black eyes, the dark complexion, and the red lips. She looks very determined."

And scary! I thought.

As we continued our tour, the professor told us about discovering Queen Tiye's tomb. "It was buried under two feet of rocks and sand when we found it," he said.

Finally, displayed in a shrine, we saw the enameled beetle that celebrated the wedding of Queen Tiye and Pharaoh Amenhotep III.

"Apparently, the Queen was particularly fond of this piece of jewelry," Professor Templeton explained. "The beetle was considered something of a lucky charm in ancient Egypt."

And bats? I felt like asking. Nobody ever talks about bats.

The professor stopped talking for a second and turned toward us. "And now, ladies and gentlemen, we are about to make this great woman's acquaintance. For more than three thousand years, her mummy has been resting in the sarcophagus that you are about to see. Don't wake her up!"

"Don't worry, I won't!" I said, climbing back into Becca's bag.

Chapter 4

Tips for Not Getting Sick

The hall that held the mummy was cloaked in darkness, except for a shaft of light that illuminated the pedestal set in the middle of the room. A large, painted wooden sarcophagus rested on top of the pedestal.

I held my breath as Becca walked closer to it. As we drew near, I instinctively closed my eyes. From inside the backpack, I heard Dr. Templeton say, "Ladies and gentlemen, here is Tiye, Queen of Egypt."

I opened one eye and found myself face to face with the mummy! Scaredy-bat!

There she was, arms crossed over her chest, wrapped in bandages that covered everything but her face and some locks of reddish hair.

"Good morning, Your Majesty!" I said, trembling.

"I say she used to dye her hair," Tyler said. "Worried about her looks, just like any other woman! Right, Echo?"

Becca immediately stuck out her tongue at him. I didn't even answer him. I was so fascinated by the idea of being in front of a 3,500-year-old queen!

"Look at her red hair," Professor Templeton said. "It

proves that even Egyptian queens used to dye their hair."

People laughed, and Tyler glared at Becca. Then he pulled out his digital camera, but before he could take a picture, the professor stopped him.

"No pictures in here!" Professor Templeton said. "The light from the flash would damage the mummy!"

Tyler grumbled, but he listened and put his camera away.

"The Egyptians used to mummify their bodies to allow the dead to continue their existence in the afterlife," Professor Templeton explained. "Mummification was supposed to make a person's body last for centuries. In a way, they became immortal!"

"Cool!" Tyler exclaimed. "Maybe I'll get

mummified too. Think about it. Tyler Silver the Immortal! Want to join me, Echo?"

"No, thanks. I think I'll pass," I replied.

The professor started explaining how mummification worked, and that was when my problems really began. It was disgusting! My head was spinning, and my vision blurred. I felt like I was about to throw up.

"Psst," I whispered. "I'm not feeling very well. Can we go out for a minute?"

"Now?" Becca asked.

"Just for a minute. I need some fresh air," I said.

"Okay," Becca replied.

Going back the same way we had come, we went outside the museum. The fresh air immediately made me feel better.

"Are you feeling okay?" Becca asked. "Should we go back inside?"

"I'd rather not," I said. "You go ahead. I'll catch up with you all later."

"Okay, if you say so," Becca said. "Don't go too far, though."

I didn't plan to go far at all. I flew to the museum garden, found myself a leafy tree, and hung upside-down in its thickest part, where nobody could see me. A minute later I was asleep.

Seeing that mummy must have scared me more than I thought, because I had a terrible dream. I dreamed that someone was mummifying me, wrapping me up tightly in long white bandages. My wings were immobilized, and I couldn't fly. I suddenly woke up. Darkness was all around me!

"Help! I'm trapped in a sarcophagus!" I yelled.

Then I realized that the sun had simply set. I felt awfully foolish. Suddenly I remembered I was supposed to meet up with my friends.

I glanced at the museum. People were just coming out. Professor Templeton stopped to talk to some visitors while the rest of the crowd wandered away. Then he left too. A few minutes later, the janitor came out, locked the doors, and left.

There was no trace of Michael, Tyler, and Becca.

Where could they be?

Chapter 5

100-Yard Dash in the Museum

At first, I thought my friends had gone home. But something told me they wouldn't have left without me. That meant that they were still inside the museum. I knew it.

I had to go in and look for them, but how? The museum was closed.

I didn't give up. Instead, I thought of something my grandmother Evelyn always used to say: *"Another way in you are sure to find, as long as you're smart and have a quick mind!"*

I took a quick look around and found an open skylight. *That's my way in!* I thought.

I took flight. Just like my cousin Limp Wing had taught me, I glided, then nosedived, and swooped right through the open skylight on my first try!

I found myself in the museum's dark, dusty attic. It was full of wooden crates, big, dark paintings, and dozens of old statues that looked

alive in the half-light. Everything was covered in cobwebs. Scaredy-bat!

Using my sonar, I made my way through the mess until I saw a ray of light coming through a trapdoor. I wrestled it open and fluttered downstairs. I found myself in one of the museum corridors.

The whole museum was dead silent. A dim light barely lit the floor.

I wanted to call out for my friends, but I didn't dare. Instead, I listened closely. From the far end of the corridor I could hear quick footsteps, followed by threatening grunts!

I flew up to the ceiling and carefully started moving in that direction. The steps were getting louder and the grunting had turned into a hoarse sound. By my grandpa's sonar! They were coming my way!

I darted into a side corridor and hid in the shadows. Suddenly, I heard familiar voices. It was the Silver kids! Why were they running?

I knew the answer as soon as I peeked around the corner. Michael, Tyler, and Becca were being chased by Queen Tiye's mummy! The mummy roared like a hungry lion and ran after them with its arms outstretched!

I knew I hadn't been dreaming when I'd seen a mummy chasing after our car a few nights ago. That mummy was alive — and she was after my friends!

Luckily for all of us, the mummy didn't realize that I was up there, hidden in the darkness. I followed the group from above, looking for a way to help my friends. Unfortunately I was too busy watching out for them to watch where I was going. I ran smack into one of the paintings hanging on the wall.

The alarm sound suddenly filled the halls of the museum. *WOOP! WOOP! WOOP!*

At the screeching sound, the mummy stopped abruptly, raised her arms to the sky, and then slowly headed back the way she'd come.

I turned on the turbo-boost in my wings and flew after the Silver kids. They hadn't stopped running for a second.

"Jeez, Echo!" Tyler exclaimed as soon as he saw me. "You sure picked a bad time to visit the museum!"

"Follow me!" I said. "I know the way out!"

I quickly led the kids to the ladder that went into the attic and through the trapdoor. Then we climbed out through the skylight and down the fire escape. Finally, we made it outside, safe and sound.

"Thanks, Echo!" Michael said. "I don't know what we would've done without you."

A few seconds later, we heard the wailing of the police sirens. They must have been alerted by the museum's alarm system.

The four of us, however, were already on our way home.

Chapter 6

An Amateur Photographer

Explaining why we were late to Mr. and Mrs. Silver was no easy task.

No one wanted to lie, but we couldn't tell the truth either. We couldn't exactly say, "You see, we were being stalked by a mummy!" That would have made them even angrier.

So Becca blamed Tyler. She made up a story about him wanting to go back to the Ancient Egypt hall to take a picture of Queen Tiye's mummy and getting lost along the way.

"Taking a picture was a good excuse!" I told Becca after we'd escaped upstairs. "I almost fell for that myself!"

"The thing is, it's true!" she replied.

"What?" I asked, turning toward Tyler. He looked down at his feet in embarrassment.

"When Dr. Templeton finished his tour, Tyler told us that he wanted to go back and take a picture of the mummy," Michael explained. "He wouldn't stop bugging us about it!"

"But the professor told him . . ." I began to say.

"That pictures weren't allowed," Becca finished. "I know. He wouldn't listen, though!"

"We couldn't leave him alone," Michael went on. "So, when we saw him sneak away, we followed him."

"I went back to the Ancient Egypt exhibit," Tyler explained. "I walked up to the mummy, pulled out my camera, and took a picture. But as soon as the flash went off, the queen opened her eyes and started chasing me!"

"We started running," Becca continued, "but when we got to the exit, we realized that the museum was already locked for the night. We were trapped inside! Luckily, you showed up when you did, Echo."

Everyone was quiet for a moment. I knew we were all thinking about how close we'd come to being that mummy's dinner!

What were we going to do? We were the only ones who knew that the mummy of an ancient Egyptian queen had come to life and was having the time of her life chasing people around the museum!

"Let's go back to the museum tomorrow after school," Michael finally suggested. "One of the posters I saw said that Professor Templeton is giving a lecture at 5 o'clock. We need to learn more about that mummy."

* * *

The next day the Silver kids and I were in the lecture hall at the Fogville Museum at 5 o'clock sharp. I was hidden in Becca's backpack as usual. We were hoping that Professor Templeton's

lecture, "The Mystery of Tiye's Tomb," would answer some of our questions.

Thankfully, the professor started his lecture right on time. "All previous attempts to find the tomb of Queen Tiye had failed," he began. "Our group decided to concentrate on the Valley of Queens. We thought it would be the most logical place to look, and luck was on our side. One night, while I was studying my notes, a large bat flew into my tent. An Egyptian fruit bat, to be precise."

When I heard that, my ears perked up. I immediately thought of my cousin Alec.

"I tried to shoo him away using my papers," the professor continued, "but I accidentally knocked over my gas lamp. My notes caught on fire! Luckily, I managed to put out the fire with a handful of sand, but I was so furious that I ran out of my tent after the bat. But when I got

outside, I saw that pest slip through a crack in the rocks."

Hey! I thought angrily. I hated to hear any bat described as a pest.

"I tried to follow him, but I couldn't fit," the professor said. "So I went back to the tent to grab my flashlight and a pickaxe to widen the opening. When I finally squeezed through, I found myself inside an enormous cave. The walls were covered with hundreds of bats! The light from my flashlight must have disturbed them, because they started to fly everywhere!"

People in the audience gasped. I swear, I'll never understand why you humans are so afraid of bats!

"Then I saw a flight of stairs on the other side of the cave," the professor continued. "It led me down into an underground tomb. When I saw the seal on the wall I knew what I'd discovered. Queen Tiye's name was carved into it. It's safe to say that I owe that bat a thank you. If it hadn't been for him, I never would have found the resting place of Tutankhamen's grandmother."

"You can say that again!" I muttered from inside the backpack.

"Do you know what the most incredible thing is?" the professor asked. "According to legend, Queen Tiye hated bats! She thought they were horrible."

They probably weren't crazy about her either! I thought. But since I was supposed to be hiding, I kept my thoughts to myself.

When the lecture was over, we waited for everyone to leave before going to talk to Professor Templeton. He immediately recognized us.

"Welcome back!" he said. "Have you been

captivated by Queen Tiye? That's what happens to everybody."

"We actually have a question for you," Michael said.

"Of course," Professor Templeton replied. "What is it?"

"We were curious," Michael said. "There are so many legends about mummies. How come there isn't a single one about Queen Tiye?"

The professor smiled at us. "Well, now that you mention it, there actually *is* one legend about her," he said. "But it's so absurd that even I don't talk about it."

"Why not?" Becca asked.

"Well, it's a very strange story," the professor told us. "Like I said yesterday, Tiye was Tutankhamen's grandmother. She saw to it that he was raised to become pharaoh from the time he was born. She traveled all over Egypt with him. She showed him every corner of the kingdom and had him trained in the many things that a king should be able to do: horse riding, archery, and table manners."

"You could use that too," Becca muttered, looking at Tyler.

"Look who's talking!" Tyler said, looking a little hurt.

The professor cleared his throat to get our

attention. "However," he continued, "Queen Tiye personally trained Tutankhamen in the most important and mysterious art. Every night, before going to bed, the queen would challenge her grandson in a game of *senet*."

"What's that?" Michael asked.

"It's an ancient Egyptian game, similar to backgammon," the professor explained. "Queen Tiye was unbeatable at it. Legend has it that the day her grandson won a game, it would be the sign that he was finally ready to become pharaoh."

"I bet I could have beaten her at this senet thing with my hands tied behind my back," Tyler boasted.

"You think so?" Professor Templeton asked. "Then you must be better than Tutankhamen himself. Rumor has it that he never defeated his grandmother."

"So what happened?" Becca asked.

"Tutankhamen became pharaoh nonetheless, and his grandmother died," Professor Templeton said. "But legend has it that ever since that day, Queen Tiye wakes up at night and looks for her grandson so that he can finally beat her at a game of senet."

"Why does she want to lose so badly?" Tyler asked.

"Because she wants to rest in peace," the

professor explained. "You see, senet isn't just a simple game. The ancient Egyptians believed that the pawns moving on the checkerboard symbolized the journey that a soul must take to reach the afterlife. Whoever wins is sure to reach the afterlife. Since Tutankhamen has never beaten her, the queen is convinced that her soul is still wandering aimlessly. That is the reason why she has been looking for him. She will never rest until her grandson beats her at least once."

We were all quiet as we absorbed what Professor Templeton had told us. Then Michael broke the silence. "Can I ask you a question, Professor?" he said. "How exactly do you play senet?"

Chapter 7

Senet-Craze

Oh, how I wished Michael had never asked that question. More than that, I wished Tyler had never learned how to play senet! Why did the professor have to teach him? And why did he have to give him the game?

From that day on, Tyler thought of nothing except playing senet. As soon as we arrived home, he was glued to the computer. Tyler is a real computer wizard! But you knew that already, didn't you?

He learned that he could play senet online against kids from all over the world. There were more than 2,000 websites for senet fans worldwide. And there were even a couple of players from Fogville!

Tyler also found out that there were national, European, and world tournaments. The International Youth Senet Championships were about to kick off, and enrollment was open until midnight.

Tyler looked at the clock. "It's five to midnight!" he yelled. "I've still got time!"

There was nothing we could do to stop him.

From that moment on, Tyler wouldn't stop

bugging us to play with him. And if he couldn't get us to play, he would play senet online. He would stay glued to the screen for the whole afternoon.

"Don't you know that staring at the screen for so long is bad for you?" I finally asked him one day.

"I know," he said, keeping his eyes on the monitor. "But none of you want to play."

"Okay, okay, I'll play," I said. I was ready to sacrifice myself, as long I could get him away from that computer.

But little by little, the game started to grow on me. I was pretty good at moving the pawns across the checkerboard.

One afternoon, I finally managed to beat Tyler.

"You were just lucky!" he fumed. "I want a rematch! Right now!"

But the rematch ended the same way. And so did the re-rematch after that and the re-re-rematch after that. To make a long story short, I beat him five times in a row.

Eventually Tyler had to face facts. "Wow, Echo! You've become a real champion!" he told me, sounding impressed.

"You're pretty good too," I replied.

"I bet we'd be unbeatable if we played together," Tyler said. I recognized the look on his face. He was up to something. "Why don't you play with me in the International Youth Senet Championships, Echo?"

"Well . . . I don't know . . ." I said reluctantly. "This game takes up a lot of time. And besides, I'm a writer."

"Exactly!" Tyler said. "You can write about how we won our first international tournament!"

Just then, Michael came to the door and peeked inside. He was holding his new novel by Edgar Alan Poultry called *The Return of the Mummy*. He had a strange grin on his face. He'd probably overheard our conversation.

"I think I have a better idea for Echo's next book," he suggested.

"What is it?" I asked.

"You could write about the time when you and Tyler defeated the mummy," Michael said.

Us vs. Her Majesty

Has anyone ever dropped an ice cube down the back of your shirt? Well, that's exactly how I felt when Michael came up with that idea.

"It's so easy," Michael said. "We're the only ones who know that Queen Tiye's legend is true and that her mummy is wandering around in search of her grandson. He has to beat her at senet so she can finally rest in peace."

"You mean *unfortunately* we're the only ones who know," I muttered.

"All it would take is one of us, disguised as Tutankhamen, to beat the queen," Michael said. "Then everything would go back to normal."

"Don't look at me!" I protested. "I'm a bat. I can't dress up like a pharaoh!"

"Who said anything about *you* doing it?" Michael asked. "I meant Tyler."

"*Me?* Forget about it," Tyler said, shaking his head. "Come on, Echo, we have a championship to train for."

I was about to flutter out of the room with him, when Michael spoke up. "You know, honestly, I don't think you're afraid of the mummy, Tyler. I think you're afraid of losing!"

Tyler and I looked at each other. I knew what he was thinking. *The two of us losing at a game of senet against a 3,500-year-old queen, like a couple of chickens? No way!*

"You know what, Michael?" Tyler said, planting himself in front of his brother. "We accept the challenge! Call Queen Tiye, and tell her we're on our way."

Less than a minute later, I was already regretting our decision. Playing a game of senet against a dead Egyptian queen — a mummy to be exact — was a pretty dangerous idea!

And that wasn't all. Tyler had forgotten that

he had to dress up as Tutankhamen. And we had no idea what King Tut looked like!

"We need to talk to Professor Templeton again," Michael said.

Becca promptly volunteered. "I'll go!" she said happily. She borrowed Tyler's camera and left right away.

In the meantime, Tyler and I started competing online in the International Youth Senet Championship. We figured it would be good training, but it was a disaster!

Maybe it was because we were so scared of the queen, but we lost all our games.

"This is going terribly," I moaned. "Tyler, are you sure ancient Egyptians didn't play cards? I'm an ace at poker!"

"If we play like this against Queen Tiye, she'll take us both out," Tyler whined.

"Both of you?" Michael said, walking into the room. "You didn't think you got to play together, did you? Only Tyler is going to challenge the mummy."

Tyler's jaw dropped. "By myself?" he said. "Forget it! No way!"

"Echo can hide under your costume," Michael said.

"Uh, what costume?" Tyler asked.

"This one!" Becca said as she walked into the room smiling proudly. Obviously her mission with Professor Templeton had been successful. In one hand, she was holding an autographed photograph of the archeologist with a note that read:

To my dear friend Becca,

You're going to make an excellent young Egyptologist someday.

Best of luck,

Dr. Templeton

In the other hand she held a drawing showing the clothes a young Egyptian prince would have worn. When I saw what Tyler would have to wear, it was almost impossible not to laugh.

Halloween Costumes

Lucky for us, Mrs. Silver was very good with her sewing machine, and she was more than happy make the pharaoh costume that Tyler needed.

The hard part was telling her what we needed the costume for without lying.

"So," Mrs. Silver said after she'd finished sewing, "the costume is almost ready, and you kids still haven't told me why you are in such a hurry."

We decided to tell her the truth, the whole truth, and nothing but the truth.

"Well, the truth is," Michael began, "we have to meet with a mummy."

"Honestly, Michael, you have such an imagination," Mrs. Silver said, laughing. "Next you're going to tell me that this mummy is alive and wants to eat you!"

"She doesn't want to eat us, Mom," Becca said. "She just wants to challenge Tyler to a game of skill."

"Oh, really?" Mrs. Silver said. "And what game is that? Who is the fastest bandage roller? Kids, you are really something, aren't you?"

She called upstairs to Tyler, who had gone to put on the costume. "Tyler, are you ready? Let's see how you look in your new costume."

Tyler appeared at the top of the staircase

and slowly walked toward us. He stared at the ground in embarrassment. Instead of his normal clothes, Tyler wore a short blue-and-white tunic that left his knees uncovered, and a pair of sandals with leather laces tied behind his calves.

Michael, Becca, and I didn't dare say anything.

Luckily, Mrs. Silver was very happy with the result. "You look wonderful!" she said as she turned to leave. "Just like a pharaoh!"

"He needs makeup," Becca said. "Ancient Egyptian men used to make up their eyes."

"No way! I'm not wearing makeup!" Tyler protested, but he couldn't stop Becca. By the time his sister's makeover was finished, Tyler's eyes were coated with dark eyeliner and blue eye shadow.

I had to try hard not to laugh. If I hadn't known that it was Tyler, I wouldn't have recognized him!

Becca also had him put on a couple of bracelets and a big medallion necklace with hieroglyphics on it.

"Where did you get that?" Michael asked curiously.

"It was a gift from Professor Templeton," Becca explained. "It's a replica of a jewel from the XVIII Egyptian dynasty."

"Perfect!" Michael said. "Let's work on Echo now!"

To tell you the truth, I had forgotten all about my role in our plan. I wished Michael had forgotten, too. "You don't want to dress me up too, do you?" I asked nervously.

"Of course not. Relax," Michael said. "All

you have to do is help Tyler beat the queen from a safe distance."

"How are we supposed to communicate?" I asked. "Telepathy?"

"You'll use these!" Michael said proudly. He pulled out a pair of headphones with a built-in microphone. "Tyler will be wearing earphones hidden under his headdress."

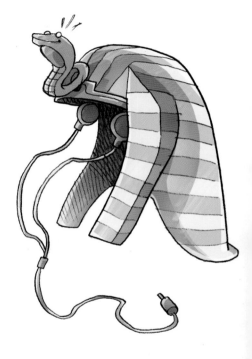

"What headdress?" Tyler asked, frowning.

"This one!" Becca replied. She held up a huge blue-and-gold-striped plastic headdress. "I found it while I was digging through our old Halloween costumes."

"But there was no headdress in the professor's drawing!" Tyler said.

"I know, but this is the only way we can hide the microphone," Becca told him. "Come on, Tyler. It'll make you look like a real pharaoh."

Tyler rolled his eyes and sighed, but he put the headdress on. We checked both the microphone and the headphones. They worked perfectly.

"Okay," Michael finally said. "I guess everything is ready."

"Are you sure that it's going to work?" Tyler asked. He sounded nervous. "I have a bad feeling about this. . . ."

"Don't worry, Tyler!" Becca said. "Everything will be fine!"

"When exactly do you plan on doing this?" Tyler asked. "You know, just so I know how much time I have left to live."

"Tonight," Michael said.

"*Tonight?*" Tyler repeated, his eyes bugging out. "Can't we wait a little longer?"

Michael shook his head. "Mom and Dad are going out to dinner tonight, and they'll be back late," he said. "We only have one chance. We have to do it tonight."

Chapter 10

To Catch a Thief

As soon as Mr. and Mrs. Silver left, we got going. When we arrived at the museum, we had to figure out how to get in.

"Can you fly up and investigate, Echo?" Michael asked. "Maybe that skylight is still open."

I immediately obeyed, even thought I was so scared that my wings felt like they were made of guano. (You humans like to say 'made of Jell-O,' but I don't really know why.)

A weak light shone from inside the museum, but it was enough for me to see that the skylight was closed. The police must have realized how we got in last time. Now what was I going to do?

There I was, flying aimlessly around, when I noticed a dark figure climbing up to the rooftop. A thief! When he got to a small window, he forced it open without making a sound and slipped inside.

Even though fear was making my wings weaker and weaker, I decided to follow him.

Not only was that guy a criminal, he could potentially derail our whole plan.

I made sure to keep a safe distance behind the thief as I followed him along the museum corridors. He was obviously pretty familiar with the place. He made it to the janitor's office in seconds and quickly opened the drawer that contained all the keys. He pulled out one labeled *Main Alarm* and stuck it into a panel full of lights and buttons.

"No alarms tonight, Your Highness!" I heard him say. Was he trying to steal Queen Tiye's mummy? Our plan was really going to the bats!

The thief walked over to the wall that held the security camera screens. There was a camera in every room of the museum.

"And no prying eyes!" he added. "Just you

and me!" He quickly turned off all the screens. Then he left and strode toward the main corridor.

I had to make up my mind fast! Did I follow the thief by myself or go back to my friends and risk losing him?

Suddenly I spotted the key labeled *Main Door*. Maybe running into that thief was lucky after all! I grabbed the key and flew back to let the others in.

Michael, Becca, and Tyler-Tutankhamen were already waiting for me outside the main door.

"Nice job, Echo! I knew you could do it!" Michael said.

"Well, I did have some help," I admitted.

"From who?" Becca asked.

I told them about the thief, how he'd disabled the alarm and the security cameras, and about my suspicions that he wanted to steal the mummy.

"We have to be very careful," Michael said. "Follow me."

"I have to go to the bathroom," Tyler whined. "Go ahead, I'll catch up with you in a minute."

"Move it, you chicken!" Becca scolded him. "You're supposed to be a pharaoh, remember?"

"Even pharaohs have to go pee," Tyler argued.

"Echo, maybe you should fly ahead and see what you can find," Michael suggested.

I quickly flew toward the Ancient Egypt exhibit and Queen Tiye's mummy. When I arrived, the thief was already there, but he didn't seem to be interested in the sarcophagus. Instead, he tinkered with the shrine that held the queen's enamel beetle.

Just then, Michael, Tyler, and Becca arrived.

"He wants to steal the beetle!" I told them.

"We have to stop him!" Michael said. "Any ideas?"

"I do!" Tyler answered. "Let's call the police and then get out of here!"

"It's too late!" Becca argued. "The thief would have time to get away."

They turned and peered around the doorway, while I fluttered above their heads. The shrine was open, and the thief had vanished, taking the beetle with him.

"Where did he go?" Tyler asked.

Suddenly, a familiar voice came out of the darkness. "Right here, kids!"

From my place on the ceiling ledge, I saw the Silver kids turn around. Behind them stood the thief. In one hand he held Queen Tiye's beetle. Reaching up, he pulled off his black mask.

"Professor Templeton!" the Silver kids exclaimed in unison.

"Ah, so you recognized me?" he asked. "You're very good! Well, actually . . .

you're very bad. You three are too young to be thieves!"

"We're not thieves!" Becca protested. "We just wanted to see the mummy!"

"That's something you'll have to explain to the police. Along with why you're walking around wearing that silly costume!" he said, looking at Tyler. "What's that supposed to be? A Halloween costume?"

"How can you be stealing such a precious artifact?" Becca asked desperately. "You discovered all of these things! It doesn't make sense!"

"Of course it makes sense," the professor snapped. "Do you have you any idea how much money this jewel is worth? Enough for me to retire on a Caribbean island and spend the rest of my life sunbathing on a beach! Just yesterday an art collector made me an offer I couldn't refuse."

"You're not going to get away with this!" Michael said.

"Oh, really?" Professor Templeton scoffed. "And how are you going to stop me? Using your ridiculous costumes?" He laughed again, glancing at Tyler. "Or are you going to use your pet bat? Speaking of which, where is he? Isn't he here to help you?"

I was still hiding near the ceiling, trying desperately to find something, anything really, that I could drop on that thief's head. Then I suddenly saw something that almost scared me to death!

"Now, here's what's going to happen," the professor was saying. "You three will stay here, while I leave the museum and lock you in. Once

I turn the alarm system back on, it should only take a few minutes for the police to arrive. Then it'll all be over for you."

The Silver kids were too stunned to answer. Now they could see what was happening behind the professor's back, too.

Two bandaged arms came out of nowhere and grabbed the professor by the arms. He turned around abruptly, and his jaw fell down to the floor. Queen Tiye's mummy stood behind him!

The beetle necklace slipped through the professor's shaking fingers. A second later, he turned and ran screaming down the museum corridor.

Chapter 11

Your "Slackness"

The mummy stood still for a moment. Then she picked up the necklace and put it around her neck. She raised her head to look at the kids, but a terrified Tyler was the only one still standing there.

Michael and Becca had disappeared.

The Queen studied Tyler from head to toe and then slowly stepped closer. She held her arms out toward him. When she was close enough . . . she hugged him, lifting him up from the ground!

"Tut! Tut! Tut! My little beloved grandson!" she cried, almost in tears. She shook Tyler as if he were a teddy bear. "Where have you been? I have been looking for you for more than three thousand years!"

Tiye had mistaken Tyler for Tutankhamen, her grandson! The disguise had worked!

"Uh, you know, granny," Tyler stammered, gaining a little courage. "I've just been pretty busy. . . ."

"I must have told you a million times not to call me Granny!" the mummy protested. "You know it makes me feel old!"

"I-is Grandmother f-fine?" Tyler stammered.

"It is acceptable, even if Splendor of Egypt would be more appropriate," the queen said.

"Let me take a look at you! Mmm, you've grown. Have you been working out? How many times do I have to tell you? A king must be in shape if he wants to be a good king. Do you understand, you bonehead?"

"Yes, Gran . . . er, Blender of Egypt . . . I mean, Smell of Doritos . . ." Tyler stuttered.

"Alas, forget about that!" Queen Tiye instructed. "Why on earth are you wearing that

horrible thing on your head? You look like a desert palm."

"It was Michael's idea," Tyler explained.

"Michael?" the queen repeated. "Who would this Michael be? The new royal tailor? What an incompetent nitwit!"

Hiding behind the column, Michael could hear every word of that conversation. Becca was with him, trying her hardest not to laugh. "Follow me," Queen Tiye commanded. "It is time to begin our evening game. And try to win, at least once! This has been tormenting me, you know? Knowing that you cannot defeat me keeps me from sleeping peacefully."

"I know that, Granny . . . err, Splinter of Egypt," Tyler mumbled.

"Will you stop that silly gibberish? Come on already,

let's set the board," she ordered. The mummy opened an ancient senet checkerboard and placed it on a table in the room.

"You may make the first move," she said to Tyler.

Tyler glanced around, looking very lost. It seemed the fear of being on his own in the company of a talking mummy had completely erased his memory!

"Well, are you going to make your move or not?" the granny — err, the mummy — asked impatiently.

I realized Tyler needed some help. I quickly put the microphone to my lips. "Pawn three on square five," I whispered.

At the sound of my voice, Tyler's face brightened and he smiled widely. He moved his pawn across the board.

"About time!" the Splendor of Egypt exclaimed. "That is a fine move, Tut! This one is better, though!" And she moved her own pawn across the board.

"Respond one move at a time," I whispered to Tyler. "Don't be hasty."

The game went on like that for a while, and the queen was leading. But I was watching the board carefully. If we chose the right moves, we could still beat her.

"You have improved greatly since the last time we played!" the mummy told Tyler. She moved another pawn across the board.

"There's our chance, Tyler!" I whispered into the microphone. "She's left one of the three exit squares open. Move the first pawn!"

Tyler didn't move.

"Move the first pawn!" I repeated. But instead

of doing what I said, Tyler kept looking around, terrified.

"Move that pawn!" I almost yelled into the microphone. But still, nothing happened. I saw Tyler tap at his ears. There was clearly something wrong with the earphones. He couldn't hear me anymore.

We were in big, big trouble!

"He's too scared to continue on his own," Becca said. "He needs help!"

"Get closer to him," Michael whispered to me. "Quick!"

That was easier said than done. I was scared too, especially now that Queen Tiye had started yelling at Tyler again.

"You will never become a great and powerful king if you keep on behaving like this, Tut!" she said, shaking her head. "A great king should be able to make the most crucial decisions without hesitation! Do you want people to one day call you 'Tutankhamen Your Slackness, the Great Wimp of Egypt'?"

"I don't, Granny . . ." Tyler stammered.

"And don't call me Granny!" the queen hollered.

"Sorry, Gran . . . err, Splendor of Egypt," Tyler said.

As usual, difficult moments made me think of my grandmother's advice: *When the going gets tough, get soft. That way you won't get hurt.*

You're probably wondering what that has to do with anything. It does, because when I decided to nosedive toward Tyler so I could whisper the next move into his ear, I was feeling so slack that I could barely stand.

Luckily for me, I just had to fly.

I took a deep breath, counted to three, and jumped!

Chapter 12

Get Him, Tut!

My idea was so simple that obviously, it . . . didn't work.

All I wanted to do was fly around Tyler's head, whisper the next move, and scoot. But as soon as I got close to the queen, she started screaming. "A bat! Help! A bat! Make it go away, Tut! Away!"

I suddenly remembered what Professor Templeton had told us. The queen hated bats. She thought they were horrible.

I glided back to Tyler. I managed to repeat, "Move the first pawn by two squares!" before gliding back behind the column.

"Oh, thank goodness he's disappeared!" the queen said, sounding relieved. "Do you know that I never dared leave my sarcophagus when I was in the desert because I was terrified of those ugly animals? They had crowded the whole cave! Then that archeologist finally arrived and took me away from there."

"Bats are harmless. Everybody knows that!" Tyler replied.

"Harmless, you say?" the queen said. "They are creatures of the darkness, and if they get into your hair, you will go completely bald."

"That's a lie!" Tyler said.

"Are you calling your grandmother a liar?" the mummy asked.

"No, of course not. I just know that —" Tyler started to say.

"You know nothing!" the queen interrupted. "Now make your move, before that thing returns!"

"I have made my move," Tyler told her. "It's your turn now!"

Queen Tiye stared at the checkerboard for a long time, a worried look on her face. In a couple of moves, all our pawns would have completed the path.

"We can't give her time to think, Echo!" Michael said urgently. "You have to go back out there."

"Again?" I asked. Part of me liked the idea of scaring someone — I'd never had a chance to do that before! But thinking about how badly that pile of rags could hurt me almost made my knees buckle.

But I knew I couldn't abandon Tyler. I had to be brave. Taking a deep breath, I took off.

"There it is again!" Tiye shrieked. "Get it, Tut! Get it!"

Tyler pretended he was trying to hit me, while I performed graceful stunts over their heads. Glides, nosedives, and finally a double loop! I even managed to graze the mummy's hair once, making her scream in sheer horror.

"Help me!" Queen Tiye screamed. "Somebody help me! I'll lose all my hair now!"

"Calm down, Granny," Tyler reassured her. "Your hair is still all there."

"I will have to call the court hairdresser right away to get an appointment," the mummy complained. She frantically patted her hair.

"Let's finish this game first," Tyler replied.

That immediately caught the mummy's attention. "Surely you don't think I'm giving up, do you?" she said. "You haven't won yet, young man!"

The same scene replayed twice. Every time the queen was ready to concentrate, Michael sent me on my mission, telling me to scare the bandages off her.

Unfortunately, the last time didn't go so well. Just when I was close enough to her to touch her nose and stick my tongue out at her, Queen

Tiye pulled a small wooden scepter out of the sarcophagus. She hit me on the head, knocking me to the floor.

"Take that!" she bellowed triumphantly. Then she strode toward me, ready to crush me with her imperial foot.

"I win, you puny cockroach!" she said as she got ready to squash me.

I was about to tell her that I was a bat, not a cockroach, when Tyler intervened. "No, my dear granny, this time *I* win!" he said.

"I have already told you not to call . . . what did you just say?" Queen Tiye asked.

"I said I beat you!" Tyler told the mummy. "My last pawn left the board, and you still have two left!"

Queen Tiye smiled and burst into tears of joy. "My dear grandson!" she said, hugging poor Tyler. "My mission is finally over. You shall become a great pharaoh! I am so proud of you, Tut! I shall finally be able to rest in peace. Farewell!"

The queen turned and slowly made her way back to her sarcophagus.

"Just a moment!" she said, stopping abruptly. "I have something I want to give to you. I've kept it safe for you all these years."

The mummy fumbled through her bandages and pulled out a small black stone beetle. "This shall be your lucky charm!" she said, handing it to Tyler.

With that, she reached out and hugged
Tyler one last time. Then she lay down in the
royal sarcophagus, closing the lid over her head.
Forever.

Chapter 13

A Lucky Charm

When the police arrived at the museum the next day, they easily discovered how the thief had broken in and disabled the alarm system and security cameras.

But they had a harder time figuring out why the sarcophagus was closed and how the enamel beetle had ended up around the Queen's neck instead of inside the shrine. They were also stumped to find Professor Templeton on the outskirts of town, running around like a maniac and talking complete nonsense.

Becca was the most disappointed of all of us. But at least she learned that you shouldn't judge a book by its cover. Even charming people can turn out to be dangerous.

The most amazing part of the story was what Tyler told us when he came home from school the next day. I was asleep in the attic, hanging upside down and trying to recover from our adventure, when he came running up the stairs.

Tyler shook me awake. He was grinning from ear to ear and couldn't wait to talk to me. He hollered for Becca and Michael to come upstairs. As soon as they arrived, he started chattering.

"It really works!" he said.

"What really works?" I asked.

"The stone beetle!" Tyler exclaimed. "Ask me what grade I got on my math test!"

"What grade did you get?" Michael asked.

"An A! I got an A!" he hollered. "Can you believe it? And that's not all. I bought candy from the vending machine in the hallway and a whole pile of stuff came down for free! Since I had extra, I gave some to the rest of my class.  Then my classmate Adam apologized for a fight we had last week, and Jenny Bristol kept smiling at me all day!"

"Jenny Bristol was smiling at you?" Michael asked, raising his eyebrow. "I'm not sure you can consider that lucky."

"You're just jealous!" Tyler replied, annoyed. "Guess what else? I just found ten dollars by your door, and I'm keeping it."

"Hey! That's the money I lost yesterday!" Michael yelled. "Give it back, you little thief!" Tyler took off running down the stairs, with Michael hot on his heels.

Becca stayed a little longer. "Have you heard from your Egyptian cousin lately?" she asked.

"I wrote him a letter, but he hasn't written back yet," I told her.

* * *

During dinner that night, Mr. Silver read us an article in the *Fogville Echo* about the end of Queen Tiye's exhibition.

"*The mummy, the statues, and the precious jewels will return to Egypt aboard a special flight leaving from the city airport at dawn,*" he read.

"What a silly idea," Mrs. Silver said. "A mummy that travels by plane."

"Knowing her, I'm surprised that she's not flying it," Tyler mumbled under his breath.

Michael, Tyler, Becca, and I all woke up at dawn to watch the queen's plane take off. Standing at the attic window, we all waved goodbye to our old friend. May she rest in peace!

One person who is not resting, or letting me rest, is Tyler. As usual. Since he started competing in the International Youth Senet Championships, he hasn't lost a game. He even organized a school tournament and won hands down!

But what's more surprising is that he keeps getting A's in math.

"That's just luck!" Michael and Becca always insist. But every now and then, especially when they have a big test, they borrow his beetle.

Oh, I almost forgot! My Egyptian cousin Alec wrote me back.

He's doing well, and told me that he was the bat that knocked over Professor Templeton's lamp that night in the desert. He said that if he'd known that he'd been responsible for such an important discovery, he would have asked

for a reward. Maybe some of those fruits and vegetables that he likes so much!

He also promised that he'd come see me. He's anxious to meet humans that treat bats as friends, rather than being afraid of them!

An upside-down goodbye,

Echo

ABOUT THE AUTHOR

Roberto Pavanello is an accomplished children's author and teacher. He currently teaches Italian at a local middle school and is an expert in children's theatre. Pavanello has written many children's books, including *Dracula and the School of Vampires*, *Look I'm Calling the Shadow Man!*, and the Bat Pat series, which has been published in Spain, Belgium, Holland, Turkey, Brazil, Argentina, China, and now the United States as Echo and the Bat Pack. He is also the author of the Oscar & Co. series, as well as the Flambus Green books. Pavanello currently lives in Italy with his wife and three children.

FAKE EGYPTIANS

Oh, boy! Look at those pharaohs! My friends dressed up as ancient Egyptians, but there's still something modern on each one of them. Can you tell what it is?

A.

B.

C.

Answers: A) Camera, B) Wrist watch, C) Ice cream cone

LET'S PLAY WITH HIEROGLYPHICS!

Ancient Egyptians used hieroglyphics, a writing system made up of different symbols. Only priests and scribes were able to use it. That doesn't surprise me, since there were 750 symbols. Not even the pharaohs themselves wanted to learn them!

Use the key on the opposite page to translate the hieroglyphics below, and discover Queen Tiye's favorite food. You might be surprised to find out what it is!

= C

 = Z

= 1

 = E

= H

= A

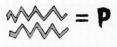 = P

 = S

Echo and the Bat Pack

THE MIDNIGHT WITCHES

Echo and the Bat Pack

TREASURE IN THE GRAVEYARD

Echo and the Bat Pack

THE THING IN THE SEWERS

Check out more
Mysteries and
Adventures with
Echo and the Bat Pack